Rosie's got a rival!

"It's that girl," Brede said, looking out the window.

"Who . . . ?" I stood up and looked out the window, too, to see who Brede meant. Julie Evans was outside with a hammer and nails and a bunch of papers.

"She's nailing something up on my telephone pole," I said. I was thinking. I knew what Julie was doing. At least I thought so.

I slowed down a little on my way down the driveway. I kept my eyes on the sign. And then I stopped.

JULIE EVANS, STAR OF <u>SWAN LAKE</u>, SAYS
SIGN UP NOW TO BE IN THE BALLET
WE WILL CHARGE ADMISSION
AND <u>YOU</u> WILL GET SOME OF THE MONEY

OTHER CHAPTER BOOKS FROM PUFFIN

Cam Jansen and the Mystery of the Stolen Diamonds   Adler/Natti

Cam Jansen and the Mystery of the Television Dog   Adler/Natti

Dance with Rosie   Giff/Durrell

Elisa in the Middle   Hurwitz/Hoban

A Gift for Mama   Hautzig/Diamond

The House on Walenska Street   Herman/Avishai

M&M and the Haunted House Game   Ross/Hafner

Meet M&M   Ross/Hafner

Rosie's Nutcracker Dreams   Giff/Durrell

Song Lee and the Leech Man   Kline/Remkiewicz

Starring Rosie   Giff/Durrell

Two Girls in Sister Dresses   Van Leeuwen/Benson

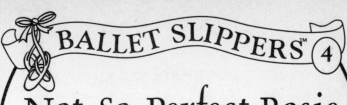

BALLET SLIPPERS™ 4

Not-So-Perfect Rosie

by Patricia Reilly Giff

illustrated by Julie Durrell

PUFFIN BOOKS

PUFFIN BOOKS

Published by the Penguin Group

Penguin Putnam Inc., 375 Hudson Street, New York, New York 10014, U.S.A.

Penguin Books Ltd, 27 Wrights Lane, London W8 5TZ, England

Penguin Books Australia Ltd, Ringwood, Victoria, Australia

Penguin Books Canada Ltd, 10 Alcorn Avenue, Toronto, Ontario, Canada M4V 3B2

Penguin Books (N.Z.) Ltd, 182-190 Wairau Road, Auckland 10, New Zealand

Penguin Books Ltd, Registered Offices: Harmondsworth, Middlesex, England

First published in the United States of America by Viking,
a division of Penguin Books USA Inc., 1997
Published in Puffin Books 1998

1 3 5 7 9 10 8 6 4 2

THE LIBRARY OF CONGRESS HAS CATALOGED THE VIKING EDITION AS FOLLOWS:
Giff, Patricia Reilly.
Not-so-perfect Rosie / by Patricia Reilly Giff; illustrated by Julie Durrell.
p.   cm.—(Ballet slippers ; #4)
Summary: A visit from her Irish cousin during Rosie's plans for a special
ballet performance proves that not everyone is perfect.
ISBN 0-670-86968-6
[1. Ballet—Fiction. 2. Cousins—Fiction.] I. Title. II. Series. Giff, Patricia Reilly.
Ballet slippers; #4.
PZ7.G3626No 1997 [Fic]—dc21 96-36985 CIP AC

BALLET SLIPPERS™ is a trademark of Penguin Putnam Inc.
Puffin Books ISBN 0-14-130060-4

Printed in the United States of America

RL: 2.4

For Anne Eisele
and Mari-joy Eisele
with love

Chapter 1

I was Rosaleen, a ballerina, in the living room. I darted, and leaped, and turned, and . . . "Out of my way, Jake," I yelled at the last minute. I landed on the couch.

"That was a *pas de chat*," I said, "and a *soutenu.*"

Grandpa was clapping, and so was my little brother, Andrew.

Jake had disappeared under the couch. Only his long black tail stuck out.

"Miss Deirdre will love it, Rosie," Grandpa told me. "I love it. It's the best ballet…"

"… The best surprise," Andrew said.

I nodded. Amy, the ballerina next door, had helped me … and I had shown the rest of the ballet class. We had worked about a million hours last week.

From somewhere under the couch, Jake was growling at me. Sometimes he was a very cranky cat.

Just then, my mother poked her head out of the kitchen door. "You have about two minutes to get to the dance studio, Rosie," she said. "And don't forget to take the flowers."

I slid off the couch, gave Jake's sticking-out tail a little tap, and went into the kitchen. A bouquet of yellow daisies was jammed into the bottom shelf of the refrigerator. So were the mustard, the mayonnaise, a bunch of cold cuts, and four jelly jars.

I pulled out the daisies and took a sniff. "They smell a little like—"

"Pickles," said Andrew, leaning against my legs.

"That's a good smell," Grandpa said.

"Well . . ." I said. Pickles are all right with hamburgers, not so hot with daisies.

I went out the door with my ballet slippers under one arm, and the flowers under the other.

I took a deep breath. Besides smelling pickles, I could smell summer. Mrs. Brockfast was cutting her lawn. She was running back and forth with the mower, making neat lines in the grass. Mr. Triola was up on a ladder trimming his rosebushes. Mr. Triola loved to trim. It was a miracle he had anything left.

School was over, and the summer was free.

I took another breath. I should have felt wonderful. I didn't, though. I felt terrible.

My friend Karen Cooper was going to a ranch for the summer. "Watch out, horses," she had said, "here I come."

But worse, much worse, Miss Deirdre was leaving, too. She was flying to Paris. After today, there would be no ballet for two months.

I had figured it out on the calendar. Two months equaled eight weeks. It equaled fifty-six days ... or—I tried to remember—maybe it was sixty-six?

I would have done the whole thing in hours, but I wasn't terrific at multiplying with two digits. In fact, I wasn't terrific at anything with math. Not like my cousin Brede. Grandpa had said she could figure out a math problem in a cat's whisker.

That was the only good part of the summer. My cousin Brede was coming ... all the way from Cornakelly, Ireland. And Grandpa had said she was perfect. Absolutely perfect. When he saw that I looked worried, he said, "But you're perfect, too, Rosie-Posie. You and your brother Andrew."

Andrew maybe, but not me. I headed for the corner, trying to practice ballet in my head. *Pas de chat* ... the step of a cat. Dart and jump and pounce.

Just then, I spotted Murphy, my best friend. He was spread out on his own lawn across the street. He waved with one hand, but he didn't get up.

He had told me yesterday he was going to spend the first day of summer vacation not thinking about anything, and not doing anything.

That brought me back to my own problem. How could I ever have a good summer without Miss Deirdre and ballet?

I took too long to think about it. I was late for the last lesson ... very late. I rushed in the door. Everyone was at the *barre* doing *pliés*. Everyone except Stephanie Witt, who was trying to do a *soutenu*. Halfway into the turn she slid to the floor.

Poor Stephanie. She was the worst ballet dancer in Lynfield.

Everyone was waiting for me. Karen was smiling, and Julie had a face like rain, I guess because the flowers had been my idea ... and so had the going-away dance for Miss Deirdre.

I swallowed. I wished I could beg Miss Deirdre not to go.

"Daisies?" Miss Deirdre was saying. "How did you know they were my absolute favorites?" She held them up to her nose for a sniff, and I saw her forehead wrinkle a little. I think she was smelling pickles.

"We have another surprise," I told her quickly. And just as quickly, we all raced to the center of the floor.

Pas de chat ... and *pas de chat* again with Miss Serena playing nice soft ballet music. *Soutenu* and *glissade derrière*, and Stephanie

Witt was dancing too close to me. I gave her a little frown, and a snap of the fingers, and . . .

I did a second *glissade derrière* . . . and crashed into her.

I took a quick look around. Maybe no one noticed. But Miss Deirdre was biting her lip a little and Stephanie was rubbing her arm in between her *soutenus*.

I did the last *soutenu* with my eyes down. I couldn't look at Miss Deirdre. I couldn't look at anyone.

Afterward when Miss Deirdre said, "Bravo, Rosie," I shook my head.

"You can't be perfect every two minutes," Stephanie whispered.

And Miss Deirdre said, "The main thing was the trying."

I nodded, but I knew I had spoiled the whole thing.

Chapter 2

The next day, we were at the kitchen table, Andrew, and me, and my cousin Brede. We were drinking milk with a teaspoon of tea, and eating scones that Brede had made with her mother in Ireland.

The scones were horrible, just as Grandpa had warned me. "You might just as well be eating horses' hooves," he had said, and winked. "Make sure you eat them, every last rock-hard bite. You don't want to hurt her feelings."

I nibbled around the edges now, trying to

bite off a raisin. At the same time I was trying for perfect table manners. Brede was using her napkin, and had one hand in her lap.

I frowned at Andrew, who was floating a lump of scone in his milk-tea, and then I noticed Brede. She certainly wasn't eating scones.

She looked up. "Hard as camels' heels, these scones."

Andrew nodded. "Grandpa said horses' hooves."

"*Andrew,*" I said.

Brede looked up at the ceiling. "Elephant's toenails."

Andrew was hysterical. "Dog—"

"*Andrew,*" I said even louder, before he could finish whatever horrible thing he was going to say.

I put my scone in my napkin while they were still laughing, and went into my bed-room.

Grandpa had moved my old bed down from the attic. It was the ugliest thing you ever saw: scratches, a painted girl on the back, and one knob dented.

"What will Brede think?" I had asked.

"You were the one, you know," Andrew had told me. "You made the scratch, and painted the girl, and dented the knob. Grandpa said."

I sighed. It was true. I tossed the scone into the wastebasket. It landed with a thud so loud I jumped.

Then I sat on the floor, legs straight out in front of me, and held on to my feet. "Nose to the toes," I said, in a Miss Deirdre voice. I did about ten of them . . . mostly "nose to the knees" . . . before I went downstairs again to the kitchen.

Nobody was there anymore. Grandpa had taken Andrew for a walk, and Brede was reading on the front steps. "It's the best book," she told me, and moved over to give me room.

She held up the book. "I'm reading it because of you. It's the life story of Anna Pavlova."

I nodded slowly, watching Murphy across the street. I'd never heard of Anna What's-her-name.

Murphy was waiting for me to call him over. He was like that—shy. He was sitting still as a stone, staring down at the grass. He was trying to find a queen ant for his ant farm. And he'd sit there for the next two hours unless I yelled for him.

Which I did. "Murphy!" I screeched, trying to figure out from the cover of Brede's book who Anna Whozit was.

Murphy took a last look around in the grass, then he ambled over.

He ducked his head at us, then lay down on the front path and began to look for a queen ant again.

I looked across at Amy Stetson's porch. She

was practicing *grand jetés* across her mother's flower pots.

I poked my head up to see her better. She was perfect. One foot followed the other, the back foot landing in the exact same spot as the front.

Amy never took one day off from ballet. Of course, Amy was fourteen and almost a real ballerina, but still...

It felt strange that I had practiced only two minutes today. What was the use, though? Miss Deirdre wouldn't be back for all those weeks, all those hours.

As Andrew would say when he wasn't happy, it was a scrambled-eggs day.

I sighed loud enough for Mrs. Brockfast to hear me from her front steps.

"What's the matter?" Brede asked.

"I want to be a ballet star..."

"Like Anna Pavlova." She tapped her book with one finger.

"Yes." So that's who the book person was.

I watched Murphy crawling around under our itchy ball tree, as Brede told me how Anna had seen *The Sleeping Beauty* when she was eight years old. Anna just knew she had to be a ballerina. "Like you," Brede said. "Andrew told me about the wonderful dance you made up…"

I opened my mouth, about to tell her it was really Amy who had done most of it. Then I shut it again.

"Why don't you dance around by yourself like Amy?" Murphy asked, pointing toward the Stetson's porch.

"Boring," I said.

"How can you dance by yourself?" Brede said at the same time.

"Yes, how?" I asked. I knew you could, but I was still in my scrambled-eggs mood.

Then I got the idea. I looked at a couple of ants wandering along my steps to see if any one of them looked like a queen . . . as if I even knew the difference. At the same time, I tried to think.

"Yes," I said aloud. "It's perfect."

"What?" Brede asked.

Murphy didn't bother. He knew I always told my ideas two seconds after I had gotten them.

"We'll put on our own performance," I said.

"Just like Anna Pavlova," said Brede.

"Exactly," I said.

Chapter 3

"Anyone-around-my-base-is-it!" I heard Murphy yell at the top of his lungs.

It was after supper, dark out now, with a sprinkle of lightning bugs here and there. Tree frogs were chirping in back of Mrs. Brockfast's garden, where the stream began.

I was hiding in back of the garage, scrunched over so Murphy couldn't find me. I was slapping mosquitoes off my legs every two seconds.

In between, I was practicing arm positions.

I loved fifth, both arms curved up and over my head. I felt like a real ballerina.

At the same time I was planning. First, what kind of a ballet performance could we do? In Miss Deirdre's class, we had done *The Nutcracker* and *The Sleeping Beauty*.

Second, who would be in it? I had told Brede about it before supper. Maybe Murphy would help somehow.

"You're it!" a voice shouted so loud my ears were ringing.

Murphy.

I *grand jetéd* down the driveway, and out to the street following him. "Murph?" I asked. "You'll help with the performance, won't you?"

He shook his head. "I don't think . . ." he began.

"You don't have to dance," I said. "I know you're too shy."

"I'm not shy."

"No, I didn't mean . . ." He was the shyest person I had ever met in my life. "We'll want to sell tickets," I told him, making it up as I went along. "We'll certainly have to put up signs, and—"

"Home free all," Brede screeched from the tree in front.

Murphy dashed down the driveway, trying to catch someone else. I went along with him. I spotted Julie ducking behind the corner of the house. I guess I took a breath or something, because it made Murphy turn and see her, too. They both raced for home base. Julie was fast. Her long brown ponytail bounced. Her sandals flapped. But Murphy was faster. He got there first.

"I can't believe it, Rosie," Julie told me. She sounded as if she was ready to cry. "You got in my way on purpose."

I shook my head. Then I realized it was so

dark she could hardly see me. "No, I wouldn't do that," I said. "I most certainly would not...."

Julie said something else, but I didn't hear what it was. Our porch light clicked on. My mother was calling. "Rosie. Brede. It's late. Time to come in."

"Coming," we both called back.

And then Brede came down the driveway, snapping her fingers. "Did you tell Julie about the ballet?"

I took a breath. Julie was a good dancer. I hoped she wouldn't want to be the star.

"What ballet?" Julie asked.

I tried to think of something we'd do. The only ballets I knew were *The Nutcracker* and *Sleeping Beauty*. I tried to think of what Amy Stetson had danced in. And then I remembered Brede's Anna Pavlova book. On the cover was a picture of a bird sailing around a pond.

No, not a pond. A river?

I remembered something else. Amy had danced in that. She had worn white feathers in her hair, and a white tutu.

What was the name of that ballet?

"We could do an Anna Pavlova thing," I said. "Duck…" I tried to think. "Duck River."

"Emmm," Brede said, "did you mean 'swan,' Rosie?"

"Yes," I said, "and I'll be the sw—"

"No thanks," said Julie. In the light from the porch, I could see her with her hands on her hips, and her bangs flopping over her forehead. I had never noticed before what a fresh face she had.

"Never mind," I said. I followed Brede up the step, opened the porch door, and banged it shut behind me.

Chapter 4

I was still in pajamas, and Brede was still asleep. I didn't have time to sleep. I had to practice.

Now I had something to practice for. *Swan Lake*.

I'd be the swan. At least I guessed I was going to be the swan. When I got my hands on Brede's Anna Pavlova book, I'd find out whether the star was a swan or a person, or whatever.

And I was going to be whatever.

Too bad the book was under Brede's pillow.
I could see a bit of the blue sticking out.

I sat down on the floor and began my flexes.
"Hello, toes," I whispered, pulling my toes
toward my legs. "Good-bye, toes," I whispered a
moment later, pushing them away.

I was dying to see Brede's book. Maybe if I
tiptoed over, and carefully …

I *relevéd* to my feet … *relevéd* quietly.

Up close I could see a bit of the swan.

I started to pull the book, slowly, gently …

Brede opened her eyes and began to scream.

"Are you crazy?" I asked her, after she had
calmed down enough to hear me.

She sat up. "I thought you were a robber."

By this time, Andrew was at the door. "I
thought you were a robber," he said.

"Never," said Brede, smiling at me.

"Never," I agreed.

We put on our clothes and went downstairs
for breakfast a few minutes later. "*Jeté* your-

selves over to the table," Grandpa said. "The sun is shining, and I have a terrific breakfast for you."

I plunked myself into a chair while Grandpa plunked down our breakfast.

"Porridge," he said, "with mushrooms on the side."

"Just like we have at home," Brede said. "Lovely. My mother puts it in a pot to soak overnight."

I didn't know how I was going to eat it. But Brede had begun already, so I put a ton of sugar on top, and poured in a lake of milk. I ignored the shriveled brown mushrooms.

Outside, then, I could hear pounding.

"It's that girl," Brede said, looking out the window.

"Who . . . ?" I stood up and looked out the window, too, to see who Brede meant. Julie Evans was outside with a hammer and nails and a bunch of papers.

Murphy was watching her from across the street. And even Stephanie Witt and one of her thousand brothers had stopped to see what she was doing.

"She's nailing something up on my telephone pole," I said.

"It's my telephone pole, too," Andrew said. "It belongs to the whole O'Meara family."

"Really?" Brede asked.

"Actually, no," said Grandpa as I moved closer to the window. "It belongs to the telephone company."

I took a breath. Stephanie and Witt Brother . . . Number Four, I think, were reading the paper on the pole. They were nodding, and Stephanie was smiling.

Even Murphy wandered over to look.

I shut one eye to see better. I could see a swan. A big white swan. Underneath was writing, lots of writing, but it was too small to see.

I went back to the table and sat down again. Across from me, Brede was eating porridge, a dot on the spoon at a time. Brede was the slowest eater in the world.

I began to eat. I didn't even taste the cereal. I was thinking. I knew what Julie was doing. At least I thought so.

I didn't move from my seat until I finished most of the gluey cereal in my bowl. Than I swiveled around. Julie was gone.

I could see which way she had walked. Papers were tacked on every pole all the way to Orient Street.

I put my bowl in the dishwasher, and started out the door.

"I'm coming," Brede said. "I just have two more bites."

I slowed down a little on my way down the driveway. I kept my eyes on the sign.

The swan got bigger and fatter.

And then I stopped.

JULIE EVANS, STAR OF <u>SWAN LAKE</u>, SAYS

SIGN UP NOW TO BE IN THE BALLET

WE WILL CHARGE ADMISSSION

AND <u>YOU</u> WILL GET SOME OF THE MONEY

I stood there a minute. Then I went back into the house. I wondered, what could I do now?

Chapter 5

Everyone had gone to Delano's Delicious Chocolates. It was because of the sale. Peppermint patties. Two for the price of one.

I wasn't that crazy about peppermint patties, but Brede loved them. She and Andrew had raced down there to be first in line. "We don't want them to run out," Andrew had told me.

Good. I had stuff to do. First I headed for Andrew's room, and dragged three of his stuffed toys out of the toy box, and set them up in the hall. I had to practice *grand jetés*.

I ran down the hall with one foot chasing the other, then leaped over the toys, right foot first. Then I turned and *jetéd* back, left foot first.

I did it about fifty times, and then I remembered the Anna Pavlova book.

I *jetéd* into our bedroom, grabbed the book out from under Brede's pillow, and sank down to read. Anna Pavlova was Russian, born in Russia, grew up in Russia. And *The Sleeping Beauty* music had even been written by a Russian man, but I couldn't pronounce his name in a thousand years.

And then I read about the swan. The biggest surprise was that the swan on the cover wasn't for *Swan Lake*, it was for a dying swan.

Anna Pavlova had made that part famous.

I chewed on my lip. Why would anyone want to see the dance of a dying swan? Never mind. If Anna could do it, I could, too.

And never mind Anna right now. I grabbed my own markers, and slid poster paper out from under the painted girl bed.

I didn't have much time to waste drawing swans all over the place. I kept it simple, and wrote out ten advertisements.

SWAN LAKE

and

THE DYING SWAN
(Mixed Together)
TWO FOR THE PIRCE OF ONE

I stepped back to look. It was much too plain. It needed pizzazz. It needed a picture or something.

I dived under the painted-girl bed again, and reached for my ballet slippers.

I spent half the morning tracing ballet slippers on the ten advertisements.

Then I stepped back again. Too bad the bottoms of the ballet slippers had been a little dirty.

The signs had black spots all over them. And they still needed something else.

I sat there thinking. Then I picked up my pen. Good thing there was room on the bottom of the paper.

WE WILL BE HAVING A RUSSIAN DANCER

Yes.

I gathered up the pieces of cardboard, and raced out the front door. Perfect.

I saw Murphy outside. "Hey, Murphy," I yelled. "Want to help?"

Murphy raised one shoulder. That meant all right.

I made a quick stop in the garage for Grandpa's hammer and nails. Then Murphy and I went to hang the signs all over Lynfield.

I wasn't wasting time anymore. On Orient

Street I *jetéd*. On Scranton Avenue I did *pas de chats*. And on the corners I did *soutenus*, twirling around the telephone poles.

For a quick moment, I thought about ripping down the signs Julie had made.

I didn't, though. For one thing, it just didn't seem right. For another, my mother was sure to find out. And my mother hated stuff like that. She'd make me put them all back up—and apologize to Julie Evans, too.

I got mad every time I thought of Julie. But wait until she found out I was having two ballets for the price of one.

With a Russian dancer.

I wondered where I was going to get the Russian dancer. I frowned a little. Stephanie Witt's grandfather had come from somewhere with an R—Russia, I bet it was. Stephanie Witt. Wouldn't you know. If only it had been my own Grandpa.

Just then I saw Brede coming down Scranton Avenue, with Andrew trailing behind.

In back of them, a Witt brother was coming along on his bicycle.

Brede was on top of us by the time Murph and I had nailed up the last cardboard sign.

She read it, head turned to one side, as I leaned over her shoulder to flick off a little of the ballet slipper dirt. "A Russian dancer?" she asked.

I opened my mouth to tell her I had just made it up. Then I remembered. Brede was perfect, Grandpa had said so. I had to be perfect, too. "Well…" I said. "Maybe Stephanie. At least I think—"

But Brede was on to something else. "It's a strange country I'm in," she said. "With the spelling different…"

"What spelling?" I asked a little nervously.

"See that?" she said. "Two for the…"

"*Pirce*," I said. I couldn't believe it. My signs were all over Lynfield, all spelled wrong.

"You can't be perfect at everything," Brede said when she saw my face.

"I know," I told her. But I couldn't say the rest. I really wasn't perfect at anything.

Chapter 6

I woke up thinking about Anna Pavlova, the ballet star.

Not so hard to be a star.

Not if you practiced fifteen hours a day.

What I needed right now was about thirty hours a day to work on splits. I put one leg out in front, and one leg in back. I tried to slide down to the floor. I got down about two inches. I rocked to get down further. All that happened was a shooting pain up and down my legs.

Anna Pavlova deserved to have a book written about her.

I tiptoed out of the room before Brede woke up. Half a sour grapefruit was waiting for me. I could see the porridge in a pot on back of the stove. I had to get out of there before Grandpa poured some into my bowl.

I headed over to the Witts' house. All of them—too many to count—were running around on their lawn. They were dodging the hose that Witt Brother Number Three was spraying at them.

Witt Number Three was called Frog. I think his real name was Frank. Frog was the best soccer player in Lynfield, the best jumper, and the best boy ballet dancer around. He was the only boy ballet dancer around.

That's why I needed him for the swan thing. I turned to watch Stephanie next. She was balleting around the lawn, arms over her head, toes pointed, her legs like marshmallows.

Poor Stephanie was the one who looked like a frog.

But she and Frog went together. Two for the price of one, like peppermint patties.

I saw Julie coming up the street. She was doing *soutenus* around every tree, but she'd be at the Witt house in a cat's whisker.

"Oh no, you don't," I said under my breath. I stepped onto the lawn—and under the hose. The spray of water plastered down my hair, and squished into my sneakers.

"Hey, Witts," I said. "Want to be in a ballet?" Frog dropped the hose. It wiggled around on its own for a minute, shooting water into their front screen window.

I could hear Mrs. Witt shout something, then someone . . . Witt Number Five maybe . . . picked up the hose. He took a quick gulp of water, then threw it behind a bush.

Frog and Stephanie were looking at each other. I could tell they were trying to decide.

41

"We get some of the money?" Frog asked.

"That's not nice," Stephanie told him.

I looked over my shoulder. Julie had two trees left to get there.

I wiped water off my cheeks. "Don't worry," I told Frog. I didn't pay attention to Stephanie. "We'll divide the money up, fair and square."

Frog scratched his ear, thinking.

Julie had one more tree.

Frog began on his other ear. "Well…"

Julie twirled to a stop at their driveway. "Want to be in a ballet?" she asked. "We'll make a fortune."

Everyone stopped to look at her. "Another ballet?" Frog asked.

Julie did a quick *plié*. "*Swan Lake* with Julie Evans," she said.

Stephanie nodded slowly. "I've got a great idea," she said. "The greatest."

I bit my lip. "What's that?"

"I don't care about the money either,"

Stephanie said. "I'll be in your ballet, and Frog can be in Julie's. That's fair and square."

Frog stopped scratching. "Sounds good to me," he said.

"Me, too," Julie said, smirking at me.

I looked at Stephanie. My two-for-one ballet was just about ruined. But what could I do?

"All right," I said. "Why not?"

The Witts were carrying on again, screaming, running. I leaned over to Stephanie. "Where did your grandfather come from anyway?" I asked.

Stephanie thought for a minute. "Rhode Island," she said at last. "Providence, Rhode Island."

Chapter 7

After lunch we started down the street, Murphy and Brede, Stephanie, and me. The whole time Brede was talking about Stephanie's grandfather, and how Stephanie must be a wonderful dancer because of where he came from, and maybe he even knew Anna.

Stephanie kept saying "*who?*" and "*what?*" and I kept saying stuff like I was dying for something cool to drink and wasn't it the hottest day ... trying to talk louder than Brede.

And then, Grandpa saved my life because

he called from our front door to say that Andrew had nothing to do.

I knew what that meant. So did Brede. "Grand," she said. "We'll take him."

"Brede," I said. "We're trying to put on a ballet here." I took a deep breath. At least Brede had stopped thinking about Stephanie's grandfather and Anna Pavlova. She was talking to Andrew a mile a minute.

It gave me time to think about what we were going to do next. I crossed my fingers as we went down the alley. We passed Delano's Delicious Chocolates and Gee-Gee's Toys and stopped at Dance with Miss Deidre.

It looked as if no one was there. I rubbed on the window to see inside, and banged on the door.

Where was Miss Serena, the piano player?

And then I heard her footsteps, and saw her loping across the studio to answer the door.

I let the whole thing out in a rush. "We're

dying to do ballet this summer," I said. "We're even going to put on a performance. We have nowhere to do it, and no music. We could pay ... Afterwards, I mean, after we sell tickets..."

"We've even got a Russian dancer," Brede said.

"Really?" Miss Serena looked surprised.

"Really?" Stephanie said at the same time.

It was a good thing Brede was jumping down the stairs with Andrew screaming in her ear. I rushed ahead. "We're going to do ..." I couldn't remember the name of the ballet.

"*The Ugly Duckling*," Andrew said, coming to a stop at the bottom step.

I nodded. "I guess so."

"Emm," Brede said.

"*The Dying Swan*," I said.

"That's pretty hard," said Miss Serena.

"Mostly *Swan Lake*," I said.

"That's not too easy, either," she said.

But it was done. Miss Serena would lend us

the studio, and even play the piano for us. "Get organized," she said. "Then I'll come out to work with you."

I nodded. I had to get organized fast, faster than Julie Evans.

I looked at what I had. Brede, who had never danced a single dance. Murphy, who was too shy to dance. Andrew, who was swinging on the *barre*.

And me, the star.

I looked around. I had almost forgotten. Stephanie Witt, who danced like a stick of wood, and who right now was slumped over a chair watching Andrew.

Brede sank down on the floor next to them. "Now you know the story of *Swan Lake*," she said. "It's simple. The beautiful princess is turned into a swan. She can't be a person again until someone loves her."

"Like a prince?" Andrew said.

"Yes, Prince Siegfried," said Brede. "But a bad

man tricks him. The Prince gets the good White Swan mixed up with the evil Black Swan…"

But Andrew wasn't paying attention. By this time, he was sliding across the floor in bare feet. I didn't even know where his sneakers had gone.

Miss Serena was standing in the doorway, eating a tomato sandwich. "You know," she said, "the part of the white swan and the black swan is the same."

"How…" I began.

Miss Serena took a bite of her sandwich. "The two are supposed to look exactly alike," she said. "In one scene she wears white, the other, black. That's how the prince gets mixed up."

This sounded even better than I had thought. Maybe we'd skip the whole dying swan business, and I could be the two swans instead.

"What you really need," Miss Serena began again in between bites of her sandwich, "is a choreographer."

"What's that?" Stephanie asked.

"The person who makes up the dances," she said.

Everyone looked at me. Andrew spoke first. "That's Rosie."

Brede and Stephanie were nodding.

Murphy was making faces in the mirror in front of the *barre*.

"I guess so," I said. I took a breath. It was going to be hard to do everything. And everything had to be perfect. "And I'll be the swans," I began.

Miss Serena shook her head. "That's too much for one person."

Brede was nodding again. "Stephanie should be the star, just like Anna."

I could see Stephanie was trying to figure

it all out. After a moment she stopped trying. She looked thrilled.

I didn't say anything. I pretended I was thinking about the choreography, or whatever it was called. How could this have happened? The ballet was my own idea, and I wasn't even going to be in it.

"You'll be lovely," Miss Serena was telling Stephanie.

"Yes," I said, and swallowed.

Chapter 8

The studio door banged open. Julie Evans came in. Behind her were Frog Witt and three other kids from our ballet class—Maureen, Judy and Ellen.

I was standing in the middle of the floor, trying to show Stephanie how to do a little *pas de chat* without taking giant steps.

"What are you doing here?" Julie asked when she saw me.

At the same time, I asked her exactly the same thing.

Julie waved her hand around. "Whatever you're doing," she said, "do it someplace else. We're practicing in here."

I poked my nose up close to hers. "Miss Serena said . . ." I began.

Miss Serena called from the little back office. "Plenty of room," she said. "One half for one production. One half for the other."

"Two for the price of one," Brede said.

Julie walked to the center of the room. She held out her arms. "This is the line," she said. "There's your side. And here's mine."

I gave her a quick nod. Then I pretended she wasn't there.

I went back to Stephanie and her *pas de chats*.

"Now look." I stood up on the balls of my feet, keeping my toes pressed down against the floor, the way Miss Deirdre had taught us.

It was hot in the studio. I could see that Stephanie's face was dripping. But she was

trying. She kept her eyes on me, nodding the whole time I spoke. It didn't do any good, though. Poor Stephanie was like a rock.

And on the other side of the room, Julie was shouting, "Great, Frog. That's great. We're the best." At the same time, she was dancing around. I guessed she was doing the White Swan.

I felt like a scrambled egg, ready to cry. I couldn't be a choreographer... I couldn't make Stephanie into a swan...

And behind me, Brede was saying, "Emmm, Rosie."

I stopped to wipe my forehead. I couldn't resist taking a quick peek across the room.

Frog was leaping up into the air, a *sauté*, and coming down lightly on the balls of his feet. Actually, I think he was making believe he was playing basketball.

I watched Julie, too, out of the corner of my

eye. When I caught her looking back at me, I turned away.

Brede was out on the floor, trying to show Stephanie what to do. "Listen, Steph," she said, her head turned to one side, "try it this way..."

And while she was talking, she was moving Stephanie's arms, pushing her feet a little with one of her own feet. "You're a swan," she said. "The White Swan. Elbows out, cross your wrists, and flutter your fingers. Move your elbows, too, just the slightest bit."

I watched for a moment. Then I crossed my own wrists and fluttered. I could see myself in the mirror behind the *barre*. Not dainty enough. I tried once more, and I could see just the way Brede was telling Stephanie to do it.

But Brede was on to the next thing. "Tickets," she told me, snapping her fingers.

"Right," I said, watching poor Stephanie say, "Like this, Brede?"

Brede looked at her and sighed. "Almost.

Now how about those tickets? Green like leaves in the springtime?"

"Yellow," said Andrew, "like the sun."

I nodded. *Like scrambled eggs*, I thought.

I went back to working with Stephanie while Brede and Andrew talked about colors.

It was impossible. I didn't know how Miss Deirdre did it. Even Brede was better at this than I was.

But Brede was disappearing up the stairs with Andrew. "Blue?" Brede was asking. "The softest blue…"

"Or purple," said Andrew. "That's even better."

They turned back to wave at me. A moment later, they were gone. Frog and the other three girls left, too.

Julie was alone on the other side of the room. She was still fluttering her fingers. No. She was wiggling them. She saw me watching her, and twirled away from the mirror.

But before she did, I saw that her face seemed sad. Julie? I must have been wrong.

I wiped my forehead. I could feel my shirt sticking to my skin. I peeled it away from my back, as I fluttered my fingers at Stephanie.

A moment later, Julie went out the door. I could hear it banging closed behind her.

Stephanie was sniffling.

"What's the matter?" I asked.

"I'm not a swan," she said. "I'm an elephant."

"You are not," I said. "You certainly..."

"Don't worry," she said. "I'll keep trying. I know you need me." But I could see she was crying.

We went up the stairs together, and let ourselves out.

I thought about the winter, and ballet, and lessons. It seemed as if the summer would last forever.

Chapter 9

I was standing with Andrew at the end of our path. We were waiting for Brede.

Finally we sat down on the curb. Andrew had a double-stick ice pop in his hand, and orange all over his mouth. Grandpa had given him the pop for eating his eggs.

I had eaten eggs, too. Grandpa had given up on the two of us as far as porridge was concerned.

I looked across the street at Murphy, and

waved. He was sitting stone still on his lawn. He didn't wave back.

But that was all right. He had warned me last night. "Don't think anything's wrong," he had said. "But I'm not going to move until I find a queen ant. I think they get worried when I jump around."

Stephanie was busy this morning, too. She was painting her garage with her father. "It's going to be perfect," she had said. "I just love to paint. But don't worry. I'll just be a little late."

I didn't mind that, either. As Brede said, things were coming along. We had our tickets ready, drawn and cut by Brede, with help from Andrew.

"Raspberry tickets," they had told me, holding them up, but they actually looked like plain pink to me.

And another thing. Last night Amy Stetson had promised to lend us costumes. White tutus and black ones, leotards and tights.

Yes, things were coming along, I thought, as I watched Andrew lean over to dribble some of his ice pop into the street.

I bit my lip. The only thing that wasn't coming along was the most important thing, the ballet.

At last Brede came out of the house. "Your face looks..." she began.

Andrew put his head up to see me. "Like scrambled eggs," he said.

Brede was smiling as we turned the corner. We walked the rest of the way listening to Andrew slurping his pop.

And that reminded me. "Why does it take you so long to eat breakfast?"

Brede shook her head. "I'm trying to be perfect this summer, and it's really hard."

"But..."

"It's the porridge. I hate it at home. I hate it here."

I swallowed, trying not to laugh. "You don't

have to be perfect every two minutes," I said, trying to remember who had said that.

Andrew licked his fingers. "Besides, Grandpa hates washing the oatmeal pot," he said.

"Really?" Brede said. "Are you sure? I'll never have to eat that stuff here again."

Then she pointed toward the studio window. "Look."

Julie had put her dance sign up on the window, and I could see that her performance was the day before ours.

Who was going to come to two ballets in two days?

Either we'd have to change our beautiful raspberry tickets . . . or give up on the whole thing.

I thought about it. Murphy wouldn't care if he sold tickets at the door or not. And Brede, who was going to be the prince—just standing around because she couldn't dance—would be thrilled to have her summer free. Stephanie could paint, and I...

I'd just wait until fall to dance again. Maybe that was it. Maybe we should just give up.

We went down the stairs. Julie was in the studio with Frog and the rest of her dance group.

Miss Stephanie was at the piano, playing soft music, swan music.

I thought about the story. The White Swan under a spell, waiting for so long to become a person again. Her wings would be moving back and forth such a tiny bit, you could hardly see them. And then when at last she was free, she'd *jeté* across the meadow, leaping, her arms stretched out...

I didn't stop to think. I forgot anyone was there. For a moment, I could feel how happy the princess was. I could see her almost flying away from the pond.

And in back of me, Miss Serena's piano music had picked up. It was fast and full of joy.

Almost without thinking, I pulled off my sneakers, and began to dance in my socks.

No one said anything. No one moved. As I twirled, I remembered to keep my eyes on one thing so I wouldn't get dizzy. "To spot," as Miss Deirdre would say.

What I spotted was Miss Serena looking over her shoulder as she played, and Stephanie Witt coming in the front door, a dab of green paint on her nose. Julie had stopped in the middle of her dance, her hands out, her mouth open, and Andrew and Brede were smiling at me.

I couldn't stop. I kept going even though I was out of breath, and my face was wet, and my socks were beginning to slide off my feet.

Then, at last, just before the music ended, I tried one last *soutenu*. I slid across the room, and landed with my head against the mirror.

I had done it again . . . wrecked the whole thing. I looked up . . . straight into Julie's eyes. I saw that she was ready to cry.

"Perfect," she said. "You're always perfect."

I rubbed my head and opened my mouth. "What are you talking about?" I began to ask.

But Julie didn't say another word. She went upstairs and banged out the studio door.

Chapter 10

Grandpa always said, "Want to make your troubles disappear? Drink cocoa in the winter, lemonade in the summer." And then he'd smack his lips.

I guess I needed oceans of lemonade.

If only Grandpa was right.

And right now Brede and Andrew were helping him squeeze the lemons. Murphy was cutting spearmint leaves in his backyard. "We'll float them in with the ice cubes," he said.

And I was on my way to a couple of places. Mr. Mooney's Crow's Nest Country Store for a box of gingersnaps, then to the Witts . . . I took a deep breath. But first I was going to Julie Evans's house.

I walked slowly. Everyone might think it was because the sun was beating down. It wasn't that. I had to take my time. I had to plan out what I'd say to Julie.

When I turned the corner, I could see her sitting on her front steps reading a book. She didn't look up when I started up the path. I cleared my throat a little.

She still didn't look up, but she knew I was there. I sat down next to her and said, "Brede ate oatmeal for days because she wanted to be perfect. And I made up that Russian dancer stuff because I wanted to be perfect, too. And . . ." I tried to think.

Julie put her book down.

"I didn't tell everyone," I said, "but Amy

helped me with the going-away dance for Miss Deirdre."

"It's hard to be perfect every two minutes," Julie said.

"That's what I think." I looked at the book she was reading, *Ballet for Beginners*, and tapped the cover. "You're great at ballet," I said.

She blinked. "I wish I could be as good as you."

"But I'm always falling, and . . ." I sighed. "Grandpa's making lemonade, and I thought you and me and the Witts and everyone could have some."

Julie stood up. "Maybe we could stick both ballets together."

"Two for the price of one," I said as we headed for Stephanie's house. "Only one thing," I told her. We *bouréed* down the street and *soutenued* around the telephone pole. "Do you know who the star of the swan thing has to be?"

She rolled her eyes. "I guess so."

We looked down the street. The star of the swan thing was on her front lawn, doing *jetés* through a spray of water from the hose. Her knees looked like jelly, her arms like rulers.

Stephanie saw us and slid to a stop. "Look," she said. She stuck her elbows out, crossed her wrists, and began to flutter her fingers.

Actually, wiggle her fingers.

Next to me, Julie sighed. "You can't be perfect every two minutes," she whispered.

I nodded. "It's the trying that counts."

I ducked under the hose for a quick cool-off, then I told everyone about the lemonade. We headed for Mr. Mooney's to buy the gingersnaps. And one last thing . . . a marker. We'd have to spend the afternoon changing the dates on the raspberry tickets.

They didn't have to be perfect, after all.

From Rosie's Notebook

Barre ("BAR") It's a handrail in front of a mirror. Hold on and warm up!

Bourée ("boo-RAY") A running step.

Choreographer ("kor-ee-OG-ra-fer") This is a person who makes up the dances.

Glissade derrière ("gli-SAHD der-ee-AIR") I love the way this looks. Start off with your feet in fifth position, right foot in front. Lean your head to the left. Slide your left foot out ... and begin to raise your arms over your head. Raise your left foot, point, then spring. As you land on your left foot, stretch your right foot off the ground. (Find a picture. It's not as hard as it sounds!)

Grand battement ("GRON baht-MA") Start out in fifth position, right foot in front. Then throw your right leg up through fourth position into the air, and back down again keeping both knees staight.

Jeté ("zheh-TAY") This is a jump from one foot to the other.

Pas de chat ("pa de SHAH") This means the "step of a cat." Jump with your knees bent, right foot first, and land on your right foot and close the left.

Plié ("plee-AY") In any of the positions, slowly bend and then straighten your knees.

Sauté (so-TAY) A jump straight up.

Soutenu ("SOO-ten-oo") A turning step.

Spotting Keep your eyes on one thing as you turn. Then you won't get dizzy.

PATRICIA REILLY GIFF is the author of more than fifty books for young readers, including the popular Ronald Morgan books, the best-selling *Kids of the Polk Street School* series, and many works of nonfiction.

A former teacher and reading consultant, Ms. Giff lives in Weston, Connecticut.

JULIE DURRELL has illustrated more than thirty books for children. She lives in Cambridge, Massachusetts.